AROUND THE WORLD

BY JOHN COY

ILLUSTRATED BY
ANTONIO REONEGRO AND TOM LYNCH

LEE & LOW BOOKS INC.
NEW YORK

CATORCE (kah-TOR-say): FOURTEEN

EVET (eh-VEHT): YES

FANGUI (fun-guay): FOUL

IL EST FORT, CE MEC. (eel ay for, ser mek): THIS GUY IS GOOD.

SAN-SI (sun-seh): THREE-FOUR

SEPT-CINQ (set-sank): SEVEN-FIVE

TAKO SE ŠUTIRA. (TAH-coh say SHOO-tee-rah): THAT'S THE WAY TO SHOOT.

VOCÊ ESTÁ BOM? (voh-SAY eh-STAH bawm): ARE YOU OKAY?

THANKS TO ALEKSANDAR GRUJICIC
AND THE STUDENTS OF PAUL AND SHEILA WELLSTONE.
—J.C.

THANKS TO OUR TEACHER, MENTOR, AND FRIEND,
DAVID J. PASSALACQUA.
TRULY MISSED AND LOVED.
—A.R. AND T.L.

Text copyright © 2005 by John Coy
Illustrations copyright © 2005 by Antonio Reonegro and Tom Lynch

Manufactured in China

Book design by HAVOC Media Design
Book production by The Kids at Our House

The text is set in Joe Kubert
The illustrations are rendered in acrylic on canvas

10 9 8 7 6 5 4 3 2 1
First Edition

LIBRARY OF CONGRESS CATALOGING-IN-PUBLICATION DATA
Coy, John.
Around the world / by John Coy ;
illustrated by Antonio Reonegro and Tom Lynch.— 1st ed.
p. cm.
Summary: Portrays a gritty game of street basketball,
"Around the world," being played literally around the world,
from New York to Australia to China, and elsewhere, and then back to New York.
ISBN 1-58430-244-5
[1. Basketball—Fiction. 2. Basketball—Cartoons and comics. 3. Cartoons and comics.]
I. Reonegro, Antonio, ill. II. Lynch, Tom, ill. III. Title.
PZ7.C839455Ar 2005
[Fic]—dc22   2004030801

ISBN-13: 978-1-58430-244-5

TO JAMES NAISMITH
FOR THE GAME
—J.C.

FOR EMILY ROSE AND ANTONIO NICHOLAS,
DADDY'S A-TEAM
—A.R.

TO THOMAS, EMMA, AND FAYE,
MY THREE POINTERS
—T.L.

JAMAL AND HIS SISTER, TANIKA, ARE PLAYING A MORNING GAME OF *AROUND THE WORLD* IN ***NEW YORK.***
YOU GONNA CHANCE IT?
CHANCE.

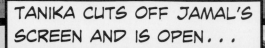

TANIKA CUTS OFF JAMAL'S SCREEN AND IS OPEN . . .

BUT SHAWN PASSES TO MALIK.

HE DRIBBLES THE BALL BETWEEN HIS LEGS AND BURSTS TO THE BASKET.

THREE GUYS COLLAPSE ON HIM.

LUC'S ON HIS LEFT AND ANDREW'S ON THE RIGHT.

SHANE FAKES TO ANDREW, THEN WRAPS THE BALL BEHIND HIS BACK TO LUC...

WHO GLIDES IN FOR A LAY-UP.

NICE LOOK, MATE.

TWO-ZERO.

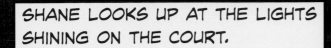

SHANE LOOKS UP AT THE LIGHTS SHINING ON THE COURT.

PERFECT NIGHT FOR HOOPS.

A SHOT GOES UP FROM THE ARC.

THE REBOUND BOUNCES LONG, AND LUC LEAPS.

HEDO CATCHES THE PASS ON A COURT IN *ISTANBUL, TURKEY.*
SWEAT SOAKS HIS SHIRT IN THE AFTERNOON HEAT AS HE DRIBBLES INTO THE CORNER.
WHUMP
WHUMP
WHUMP

AT THE NEXT HOOP, MEHMET SHOOTS ONE-HANDED.

HE'S OUT SIX MORE WEEKS WITH A BROKEN ANKLE, AND IT'S KILLING HIM NOT TO PLAY.

HEDO FLICKS A JUMPER.

EVET!

YES!

MEHMET SEES THE BALL SILHOUETTED AGAINST THE SKY.

IT LOOKS GOOD ALL THE WAY.

OBINNA AND MICHAEL PLAY TOUGH DEFENSE IN *LAGOS, NIGERIA.*

OBINNA WIPES HIS FOREHEAD WITH HIS SLEEVE IN THE HUMID HEAT.

HAKEEM CATCHES A PASS ON THE BLOCK.

HE SPINS LEFT, RIGHT. . .

FAKES. . .

AND GOES UP AND UNDER.

ON A COURT IN PARIS, FRANCE, JÉRÔME SLAPS THE REBOUND.
FWAPP!
HE TOSSES TO ANTOINE, WHO JETS UP THE FLOOR.
ANTOINE HERKY-JERKS A MOVE THAT FREEZES HIS MAN . . .
THEN GLIDES IN FOR A FINGER ROLL.
IL EST FORT, CE MEC.
THIS GUY IS GOOD.

SEPT-CINQ.

SEVEN-FIVE.

ON DEFENSE, JÉRÔME DIVES TO THE POST AND TAPS THE PASS AWAY.

ANTOINE SCOOPS UP THE BALL AND SPRINTS DOWNCOURT.

HE STOPS AT THE ARC, FAKES A THREE...

AND ZIPS A ROCKET TO JÉRÔME...

WHO GOES TO THE HOOP.

STEVE SMASHES INTO RICK'S SCREEN AT A HOOP BESIDE THE ROAD IN PATRICK'S COVE, CANADA.
KKRAK!
CALL OUT THE SCREENS!
STEVE SWARMS RICK ON A DOUBLE TEAM. . .
AND SLAPS THE BALL OUT OF BOUNDS.

TANIKA'S GUY POUNDS HIS DRIBBLE AS HE BACKS HER DOWN.

TANIKA TIMES HER MOVE, SLIDES LEFT, AND STABS AT THE BALL.

JAMAL DIVES FOR IT.

A HAND TAPS IT TO THE CORNER.

JAMAL'S MAN IS WIDE OPEN.

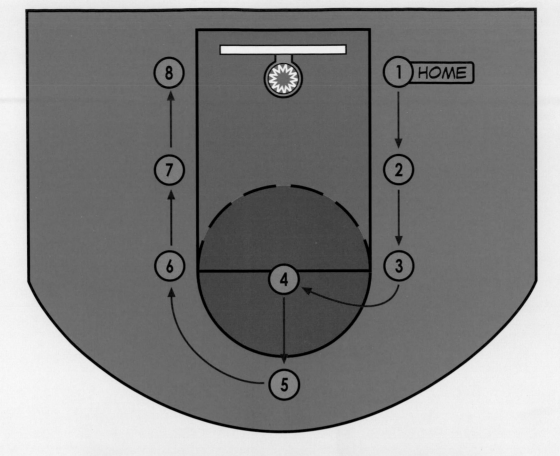

PLAYING AROUND THE WORLD

YOU'LL NEED A HOOP, A BASKETBALL, AND ANOTHER PLAYER.
THE OBJECT OF THE GAME IS TO MAKE A BASKET AT EACH SPOT AROUND THE WORLD.

SHOOT THE BALL FROM SPOT ①, ALSO CALLED HOME.
IF YOU MAKE THE BASKET, MOVE TO SPOT ②.
IF YOU MISS, YOU CAN "CHANCE IT" AND SHOOT AGAIN.
IF YOU MAKE YOUR SECOND SHOT, MOVE TO SPOT ③.
IF YOU MISS, IT'S THE OTHER PLAYER'S TURN.

KEEP ADVANCING AS LONG AS YOU MAKE YOUR SHOTS.

IF YOU MISS YOUR FIRST SHOT FROM ANY SPOT, YOU CAN PLAY IT SAFE AND WAIT
  FOR YOUR NEXT TURN.
OR YOU CAN "CHANCE IT" AND SHOOT AGAIN.
IF YOU MISS YOUR SECOND SHOT, GO ALL THE WAY BACK TO THE BEGINNING, SPOT ①.

WHEN YOU REACH SPOT ⑧, YOU ARE HALFWAY AROUND THE WORLD.
NOW YOU NEED TO MAKE SHOTS TO RETRACE YOUR PATH BACK TO HOME.

VARIATIONS:
MOVE SPOTS FARTHER FROM THE HOOP IF YOU WANT A GREATER CHALLENGE.
GIVE THE SPOTS ON THE COURT NAMES OF COUNTRIES.

MAKE SHOTS. TAKE YOUR CHANCES. HAVE FUN PLAYING AROUND THE WORLD!